For Arnold

—V. H.

For Kathryn Olivia May Harper

—B. M.

When Birds Could Talk & Bats Could Sing

THE ADVENTURES OF BRUH SPARROW,
SIS WREN, AND THEIR FRIENDS

Told by Virginia Hamilton

Illustrated by Barry Moser

THE BLUE SKY PRESS

An Imprint of Scholastic Inc. • New York

THE BLUE SKY PRESS

Text copyright © 1996 by Virginia Hamilton

Illustrations copyright © 1996 by Barry Moser

For information regarding permission, please write to:
Permissions Department,
The Blue Sky Press, an imprint of Scholastic Inc.,
555 Broadway, New York, New York 10012.

The Blue Sky Press is a registered trademark of Scholastic Inc.

Library of Congress Cataloging-in-Publication Data
Hamilton, Virginia.
When birds could talk and bats could sing:
the adventures of Bruh Sparrow, Sis Wren, and their friends/
by Virginia Hamilton; illustrated by Barry Moser.
p.   cm.
Summary: A collection of stories, featuring sparrows, jays,
buzzards, and bats, based on African American tales
originally written down by Martha Young on her father's
plantation in Alabama after the Civil War.
ISBN 0-590-47372-7
1. Afro-Americans—Folklore.   [1. Tales—Southern States.
2. Afro-Americans—Folklore.   3. Folklore—Southern States.
4. Birds—Folklore.]   I. Moser, Barry, ill.   II. Title.
PZ8.1.H154St   1995   398.24'528'08996073—dc20
95-15307   CIP   AC

12 11 10 9 8 7 6 5 4 3 2 1   6 7 8 9/9 0 1/0   46

First printing, March 1996

Contents

When Birds Could Talk
&
Bats Could Sing

How Bruh Sparrow and
Sis Wren Lost Out

Bruh Sparrow was feeling good this one fine day. And, small as he was, he knew a trick or two. He had already beaten Bruh Buzzard out of his hilltop potato patch. Yes, and now he was strutting around the fields and prancing up to the fence corner. He was just as big-acting as he could be. He sure was.

Since the time Sis Wren learned she was most fit for the fence corners, the fence corners had been her home—and Brown Wren's and Winter Wren's, too. All the wrens.

And right next, Bruh Sparrow came upon two little wrens inside the worst quarrel about something they'd found.

What did they find, and where did they find it? Well, here's the story.

All the wrens were fluttering about, jerking and jumping. They were scratching in the ground, trying to bring up something that was buried there but peeking out. And one wouldn't allow the other to scratch up what it was. Bruh Sparrow didn't have any business there or fooling with fussing families. But he did love a fuss when the folks fussing were littler than he. So Bruh Sparrow just flew right into the quarrel, quick as he could.

Suddenly, there came a cloudburst just as loud as umpteen-hundred wet wings flapping. It was a regular swish-swash of rain, a real gulley-washer, too. And still the birds couldn't scratch what it was out of the mud and wet. None of them could scratch any deeper than the high they could fly, don't you know. And not nary a one of them, wrens or Bruh Sparrow, had any idea what was buried down there.

But soon as it got warm in spring, whatever it was began to sprout. It grew and it grew some more. It twisted and turned over, and it wound itself around in a vine. That vine stretched clear across the field.

It took a whole day for the birds to get from one end of it to the other. For true! The more it grew, the more the bunch of wrens and Bruh Sparrow quarreled about it.

The whole spring and
summer and into the first frost of fall,
they were still having words.

"Give it to me. Me! Me!" cried Sis Wren and her company.

"No, it's mine," answered Bruh Sparrow with his kind.

"This vine is ours!"

A little pumpkin was growing on that vine, and getting bigger. The frost came again and fell upon the pumpkin. The pumpkin turned yellow gold and sugar sweet. It grew to be a grand pumpkin under the harvest moon. Yes, it did.

Now, not one of the small birds had seen a pumpkin before. But they had the idea that what they were seeing was worth something.

Bruh Sparrow was on the far side of that golden eat-good, and Sis Wren was on the near. Neither could see the other, the pumpkin was so wide. But they each said, "It's mine! That vine is mine." And they fussed, "Give it to me! It belongs to me!"

Yet, not Sis Wren nor Bruh Sparrow nor any of either's company took up the pumpkin. No, indeed. It's no good when something's so big you can't carry it off on your palm or in a kerchief.

Now, Captain Crow, he came by and heard the fussing. He stopped to settle things down. He figured it this way: "The seed belonged to Sis Wren. But Bruh Sparrow hid it. Then—"

The birds broke in, "Sis Wren got it. Bruh Sparrow sought it."

Captain Crow seemed to settle it. "He that can tote it—I wrote it—it belongs to him."

Well, all the birds tried, but none could carry the pumpkin. It was too big, and they were too small.

But then the youngun Alcee Lingo came along. He'd never seen anything like a pumpkin. Yet, he knew all about birds and could talk to them.

"Morning, wrens and sparrows," he said. He leaned over and thumped the pumpkin. Said, "What's this Alcee Lingo's found?" And said, "It's round, Captain Crow. Must be worth something. And I found it."

With that, Alcee tore the pumpkin from the vine. He held it in his arms and strolled on off across the field. Sadly, Sis Wren and Bruh Sparrow watched him go.

Captain Crow said, "You can close the book on that pumpkin Alcee Lingo took."

All the birds had lost out. And 'til now, pumpkins have been vine-grown for picking.

So, children, here's a leaf from the book of birds: *Pick on your own size. For it's no use squabbling over what's too big for you to handle.*

Still and Ugly Bat

Now, you know Miss Bat today, all still and ugly and off by herself. But time was when Missy Bat had a long tail and seven coats of feathers. Every coat was a different color. And she could sing just like a nightingale. Oh, she could step so high! And sing! And fly like a bird!

Her type, which was once the highest way back when, is the lowest kind today. That's it. Miss Bat had it all, way back then. She was the most beautiful of bats. Yet she liked to call herself a bird, what with her long tail and all them coats of feathers. She looked just like a beauty bird. The whole day was happy to see her fly and sing and sing and fly.

The birds planned to name her Queenie of Us All, even though she was a bat. Well, it was then Miss Bat's head got turned around. She was sitting there swaying at the top of the pine tree. Bird folks flew by singing:

> *"Pretty Miss Bat, she's like no other bird*
> *we ever heard singing.*
> *And she is better than any bird*
> *we see just winging!"*

Miss Batty, she began twirling around at the top of the tree. And her poor head turned clear around. "I won't be like everyone," she sang. "And I won't be like anyone."

Just then, the woodpecker with his crest so high came over-by. Miss Bat hollers:

> *"I won't be like him,*
> *diddle-de-dim!"*

"There." She shook the waving tuft right off the top of her head.

The redbird flew by, all sharp-looking
in the breeze. But Miss Batty had to sing,
"I'd rather be deader than redder."

"There!" She shook off the first
of her seven coats of feathers.
That was the red one. "Whew!
Feel feather-better already," she said.

Next came flying the prettiest bluebird you ever saw.
Silly Batty had to sing real strong:

> *"I'll always be different from you,*
> *for true.*
> *I'll never, ever be blue!"*

And she tore off her second coat,
which was as blue as the sea and sky
put together.

Flatter-flitter, the rice bird, fluttered by,
all little and yellow as a sun streak.
It made Miss Bat real mad to see
the bitty golden bird.

> *"I won't be yellow, I know that.*
> *Yellow coat, scat!"*

Missy Bat wiggled out of that color coat.

And wouldn't you know it? The peacock came by just then. He with his wide wings and tail spread in such pretty colors. A bird as green as a field of spring corn. But Batty didn't have the sense she was born with. She started a loud sing-holler:

"Get along with you! Can't let it be seen
that a bat's wings ever are green."

Off came her green-feather coat.

The chattering blackbird
came slattering by. Then another black
and sleek bird. And another swift, black, and
quick bird. Miss Batty's head was so turned she'd
never get it on straight again. And she began shrieking:

"Get away, Blackbird!
I won't let it be heard
that Miss Bat ever looked like that."

She slid out of that feather coat. And hopped
up and down at the very treetop, hollering at birds going by:

"I won't be like you, green, yellow, blue,
black, or brown, too, I will not be like you."

She slipped out of a brown-feather coat.

15

Next, a dove so lily-light floated by. Miss Crazy Bat, she was down to her last coat. And it was all white. She couldn't help herself, she had to sing out loud:

"I'll be black as night
before I'll be white!"

"There!" Poor Miss Bat. She tore off the last coat, all white.

She was down to skin and bone! Bone and skin! She did not have even a pin feather on. Just some short hairs all over.

Now she thought the evergreen tree she was perched on wasn't good enough for her to nest, don't you know. Nor the woods fit for her to rest. Not even daylight could suit her.

Poor Batty, she fluttered around and around, just beside herself. Right next, Mister Man happened to see her and felt sorry for her, too. Man opened the attic of his house. Miss Bat could rest there if she wanted to. He slid open the way to the barn loft so she might nest there if she had a mind.

Miss Bat chose the barn loft. Flutter, flutter, fall down! She started in crying and crying, until she cried her eyes out. Yes, she did too! And she's blind 'til now. She has to fly at night 'til ever. For she's so ugly, she's ashamed to be seen in sunlight.

Poor Miss Batty! She's bare-skinned 'til yet, like a plucked chicken. And almost sightless, hardly no light.

I know it for a fact, children, *that what is up must come down again. Stars do fall.* All right, then! Try to remember that, when you think on Miss Bat.

Blue Jay and Swallow Take the Heat

Was a time when Firekeeper had it all. Nobody else had a bit of fire, not even that Alcee Lingo, who was a find-out child always into everything. But this time, Alcee Lingo was cold with the chills. And he was all alone, the only boy in the whole countryside.

There was no fire in all the world to warm Alcee Lingo except that owned by mean old Firekeeper—didn't have any last name. And he didn't like Alcee Lingo on account of Alcee hanging around trying to warm his hands and then running away real fast when Firekeeper tried to catch him. Firekeeper wouldn't like any other child when it came into this world, either. Just awful, he was.

It got so cold that even Bruh Blue Jay felt sorry for Alcee Lingo. "That child doesn't have feathers to warm him," he said one day to Sis Blue Jay.

So Bruh Blue Jay flew off.

He had to be swift if he was
to take some fire and then get
away. So he did it. But that quick-eyed
Firekeeper saw him. He ran after Bruh
Blue Jay in a flaming rage. And scared Bruh
Blue Jay half to death. Bruh Blue Jay opened his mouth
to warn all the birds that Firekeeper was burning mad,
and—whoops!—he dropped the chunk of fire he'd taken.

"What business you have to take my fire?" Firekeeper yelled
up at him.

Scared to death, Bruh Blue Jay hollered down, "It was only

for Alcee Lingo. I'll pay, I'll pay, yes, I will! I'll pay you!" And until right yet, Bruh Blue Jay can be seen every day and most always taking stick pieces and fine little wood chips, nice and clean, over to Sis Squatty, old Firekeeper's wife.

All the time they were hollering and calling back, Miss Swallow was floating along in the free air. She grabbed up the chunk of fire Bruh Blue Jay had dropped. It was fading, but it still had glows inside it, and it felt red-hot in its heating way.

Why, Miss Swallow was such a beauty bird in those days. She could walk on her two feet. She could run or fly. She could swim and go as many ways as there were to go. She knew that the fire-hot had to be quenched some. It had to be burned out a little before it could be used by Alcee Lingo. And that had to be done seven times in seven separate ponds. For Firekeeper's heat was just too hot-full for humans.

Miss Swallow landed in the first pond she came to. Firekeeper was still yelling and shaking his fist at Bruh Blue Jay and not paying attention to Miss Swallow at all. And Missy, she headed on to this next pond as fast as she could fly. She was in and out of five ponds, with the chunk of fire in her mouth.

21

Each time she swooped into a pond and wet the chunk, the fire-hot got a bit less heated.

Miss Swallow might've got through all the ponds safely if it hadn't been for that old Sis Squatty. She happened to see what Miss Swallow was doing. She saw Miss Swallow flash out of the sixth pond. Sis Squatty took off after Miss Swallow with a red-hot poker. She did too!

There! She caught Miss Swallow still low enough and hit her on her two feet—ploom-ploom! Hurt poor Miss Swallow. Her feet have been shriveled up and weak ever since. And they can't carry the weight of Miss Swallow at all, since that day.

Good Miss Swallow wasn't about to be outdone. She flew into the last pond. The fire was now cooled seven times.

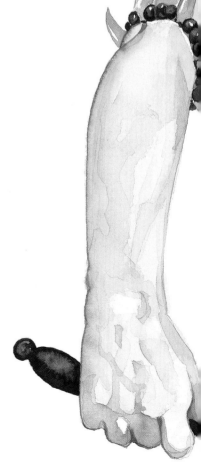

Firekeeper couldn't help hearing what was going on. Old Sis Squatty was just scolding and scolding Miss Swallow as loud as she could. Firekeeper ran after Miss Swallow with his past-hot shovel and flung it at her. Got her! The ends of Miss Swallow's tail feathers were singed by the shovel's sharp-hot edge.

Well, never you mind. The lick did help Miss Swallow, at the last. Now she can rest sometimes by poking the end of her tail into a chimney or by leaning it against a wall. It helps her get off her weak feet and snatch a little rest.

But then, Miss Swallow forgot about her tail-hurt and took that chunk of fire on over to Alcee Lingo's house. She dropped it for him at his door.

Ever since, children have toted fire chunks from cabin to cabin. And since the day Miss Swallow first carried fire to the hearth, she has floated around chimneys where it's warm. That's why we let Miss Swallow be free to build nests up there. Because we all are pleased with her. We are! And you be pleased, too, children, just like Alcee Lingo is always pleased that Miss Swallow brought him fire. Remember Bruh Blue Jay, too. He was brave to take on old Firekeeper. And: *Never you forget who took pains for us so we could stay warm.*

Bruh Buzzard and Fair Maid

Fair Maid had been a racehorse when she first came to the big farm with its meadows and fields. Alcee Lingo lived on the farm and tended to the horses. He also talked to all the animals and understood the birds. He gave Fair Maid the best of care even though now her prize-running days were over. Fair Maid was skinny and tired and on her weak last legs.

Bruh Buzzard had his eye on Fair Maid. He saw her growing slower and sadder every day. He called down to Alcee Lingo:

> *"If your Fair Maid won't slide down quick,*
> *her bones will be no good to pick.*
> *Give the poor thing over to me,*
> *and I give you fifteen dollars, clear and free."*

"I won't sell her to you," Alcee Lingo called back. "I wouldn't sell Fair Maid for any price."

"I'll just wait," said Bruh Buzzard. "And then I'll get her for nothing."

Bruh Buzzard bided his time for a week. Then, he came back to where Alcee Lingo was plowing along with Fair Maid hitched to the plow. The mare pulled slowly, but Alcee never whipped her or made her work fast. Fair Maid moved as long as she felt like it. When she couldn't move anymore, Alcee Lingo let her quit and go to the meadow to eat.

Bruh Buzzard called down to Alcee:

> *"Horsey-dorsey-moans,*
> *I'll pick her bones! Fair Maid will be mine*
> *between three years and nine."*

Well, those words worried Alcee Lingo so, that he took Fair Maid and led her three days' journey to the deep swamp. When he got there, he looked up above. Sure enough, there was Bruh Buzzard just floating on the breeze, waiting for him.

"Flop! Kerplop! Wait, son, wait!" yelled Buzzard. "Fair Maid's going to be mine, Lingo!"

Alcee Lingo threw swamp mud as high as he could. But he couldn't reach Bruh Buzzard. All he did was get mud in his own face. "Puh-tooey!" he muttered, and spat out swamp water.

Bruh Buzzard hollered down as he flew off:

> *"Ooogily-moogily,*
> *I'll pick her bones! Fair Maid is mine*
> *between three years and nine."*

Alcee Lingo took Fair Maid by the halter and led her three long days' journey to a hollow between two green hills. He knew Bruh Buzzard wouldn't find them in that place. When Alcee got them to it, he looked up to tell the time by the sun's position. And there was Guess Who. Yes, it was, and he was hanging like a black scythe against the blue. Bruh Buzzard flapped his wings and hollered at Alcee Lingo, "Wait, son, wait! Ten years and longer."

For seven hard years, Alcee Lingo led Fair Maid over the countryside. Every time they would stop, Bruh Buzzard would be up there, like a black moon in full daytime. And hollering, "Wait, son, wait! Ten miles and farther."

By now, Fair Maid was worn out. She dropped in the field. Alcee saw that she'd taken her last step. He thought she'd died. And, sadly, he went off for an hour to grieve her. When he did, Bruh Buzzard dropped down. He landed close to Fair Maid. And he whispered in her ear, "Wait, son, wait! Seven years and nine. You, Fair Maid, are mine!"

But Fair Maid had one last strength. And with it, she lifted her behind hoof and flashed it out against Bruh Buzzard's head. *Ker-buzz-it!* The blow knocked the top off that ugly bird. He's been baldheaded ever since.

So, children, hear what I say: *Never try to take advantage of the poor and weak. For the last lick they've got will surely do you in!*

Hummingbird
and Little Breeze

This is the tale I'm telling you. It's about Hummer, the hummingbird, and the day she got on the wrong side of the summer wind.

Hummer was the smallest bird in all the hummingbird family, but none of the other birds ever picked on her—for Hummer had the fastest wing-beat of any one of them. And you know all hummingbirds can fly backwards. Well, Hummer could fly backwards faster than fastest. Yes, she could! And she was pretty as she could be, with her long bill—thin enough to sew the sheerest hem. Her feathers glowed with bronze-green light.

Hummer's throat and the tips of her wings had pearly white feathers. Oh, she was a sight, flitting around the garden wall, looking for nectar from the flowers.

All the other birds loved to see her. And this one morning, they called out to her, "Morning, Hummer. We know it's going to be a fine day when we see *you*!"

Well, right about then it was that Hummer felt Old Wind pass along the garden path. "My!" she said. "Where'd you find your scent of flowers?" But the wind went on, too big and wide to waste time talking to a little hummingbird.

Hummer followed Old Wind to find his garden of flowers. See how he blows and where he goes, she thought.

A wiggle of air named Little Breeze scrambled off Old Wind and tripped Hummer. "Gotcha last, Hummer-dingy!" Little Breeze said, and took off after her granddaddy, Old Wind.

"Oh!" cried Hummer. She fell down hard on the path. But nothing could keep her down long. Hummer beat her wings as fast as they would go. They were just a blur on the air.

"Calling me names!" Hummer cried. Her only injury from the fall was her pride. In no time, she was right on Little Breeze's left side. And then, she was in her stream, just coasting, getting a good glide for free.

Little Breeze didn't like any bird that close to her. She knew that Hummer was the only bird light enough to ride her.

"I don't like you," Little Breeze said. "I'm going home, too!" And she took off in a streak so fast she left Hummer beating her wings against hot summer air.

"Where'd she go? Where's her home?" wondered Hummer.

Well, Hummer flew this way and that, hunting Little Breeze. It wasn't long before she came upon Old Wind's house, way down at the garden's edge near the meadow. She just stumbled on inside. And lo, there was such a rustle and tustle in Old Wind's place.

Wind tossed Hummer this way and that. "What d'ya think you're doing in here?" he hollered. Scared Hummer half to fainting. She heard Little Breeze giggle nearby. But she didn't have time to search for her.

Old Wind swung Hummer yonder and roundabout. He

whirled her and twirled her until her head got dizzy. 'Tis true!

"Please, sir, let me go! I won't come here anymore!" Hummer fairly sang out in her high, honey-sweet voice. Oh, it was a lovely sound she always had, too.

Just as soon as she sang the words, Old Wind blew Hummer's song clear away. Then it got so mixed up in Wind's gusts that Hummer couldn't breathe her song back again.

What came next, Old Wind lifted and scooted her right out of his house. Hummer heard Little Breeze call after her, "I'll keep some of your song, too! So there!"

Old Wind whirled her so swiftly that Hummer caught some of his rustlings on her white wing tips. And she has that whirring of the wind until today. Sounds just like soft silks rubbing together, too.

All the birds crowded around Hummer when she came whizzing down the garden path again.

"What'd you see?" Redbird asked. "We saw you go in Old Wind's house."

Hummer wanted to tell about Old Wind and Little Breeze. She spoke, but no sound came. Her voice was gone for good.

So that's the lesson, children: *It never pays to pry and spy in other folks' houses. So be careful, and mind your own business!*

When Miss Bat Could Sing

Here comes Miss Bat again. Time was after she lost her pretty feather coats and was living in Mister Man's barn loft.

All the birds still cared about the poor, skinny thing, even though she was awful full of herself. Too overbearing, if you ask me. But in those days, Miss Bat still could outsing all the birds. And thought herself a better bird than all of them. She made up the prettiest ditties and sang them all herself.

She opened up like a music box: "Click!" She wound up and let loose with one sweetness melody after another. All the birds went flocking to Mister Man's barn loft to hear her. It was one big fowl-in, so I heard.

Young Miss Field Lark got there first, just as Miss Bat commenced to sing,

"Laziness gonna kill you! Kill you!"

Miss Field Lark thought the tune sounded so special, she joined in. That got Miss Bat real mad at Miss Field Lark.

She flung the song right out of her mouth. So that gives leave for Miss Field Lark to just fly away with the song. And she did. Then comes Miss Sparrow. Miss Bat was singing away,

"Twee-ree! Twee-ree!"

Well, Miss Sparrow dipped her wings and swung around in a ballet dance and sing-along. Miss Bat got upset again, and she shot the song off her tongue. And Miss Sparrow took it up and went off with the tune and doing the ballet both at once, don't you know. And still doing that song. Always will, guess me.

Next came Mister Swallow, fluttered by first. Then he dashed this and that way. Getting near Miss Bat, he hears her:

*"Come, Summer, come along.
Here my singsong, sing-along!"*

Miss Bat had the lead on that one, and Mister Swallow came in on the follow. Made Miss Foolish Bat so mad, she flicked the song off her bill. Did too!

For she wouldn't sing any tune that
another bird could carry. Just willful.
So Mister Swallow dashed on by. He
carried the lead with him and the follow, too.

Miss Mockingbird, she come on by. She, so light as her
singing. But Miss Bat was singing oh, so much lighter, like this:

"Dixie, Dixie, do!
Never you mind some weather,
Just so the wind won't blow me over."

Well, Miss Mockingbird reeled the song off as pretty as you please.

Then Miss Bat sang:

"Day's breakin', hoecakes bakin'.
Mama! Mama! Put on the lid!
Sister's gonna make some shortnin' bread!
Oh, my, child, thought you was a-bed,
But there's you, reachin' for shortnin' bread!"

43

Miss Mockingbird caught that song on its bounce, like it belonged to her.

But that was the last of it. Miss Bat flung that one away, too. And flung every song off her bill forever. All the other birds picked them up, and each left with a song all its own.

So right now, Miss Bat sits all day long in the darkest corner of Mister Man's barn loft. She's up there as quiet as a mouse.

She is worn-out ugly, and very still, too. When night comes, she scoots on out of there while the birds are asleep. She shoots up, bare-winging, and she skims around half the night. And if you come near her, she squeaks. That's all she can do. Squeaks, "Cheat! Cheat! Cheat!"

Squeaking is all she's got left. I wouldn't lie to you. That's what I heard. Well: *It never does a body a bit of good to be hoity-toity. For pride has a way of taking a fall every time. So children, be extra careful you don't trip over yourselves!*

Cardinal and Bruh Deer

Once upon time in the forest, the boom of a hunter's gun went: *Pow-ow!* And Bruh Deer fell down. The *pow-ow!* burst all in Bruh Deer's face. Bruh Deer's legs buckled from the shock, and his head skidded into the ground. All the skin came off his face, too.

Just then, that handsome bird, Cardinal Gray, came along, flying fast and low.

He said:

> *"Wheat, wheat, wheat, who's lying there*
> *with his white tail in the air?"*

"It's me!" cried Bruh Deer. "Come on in here, Cardinal Gray. I'm hurt."

Cardinal Gray perched himself beside Bruh Deer. "You sure look a mess, but it seems like you're not hurt deep," he said. He took his wings and cleaned up the blood-red that *pow-ow!* did on Bruh Deer's cheeks and such.

"There. Now your face is all white, the way it's supposed to be," Cardinal said.

"Thank you, son," said the deer. To see somebody cared about him gave Bruh Deer courage. He scrambled to his feet. And staring at Cardinal Gray, Bruh Deer spoke up. "Son, you have changed! You are all over *red*, like the last sun going down!"

And so it happened. Ever after that gunshot, Bruh Deer's face has been white, and the cardinal has been red all over from wiping the bloody cleanup with his feathers.

Well, Cardinal Red, as he's called now, went on through the woods back to his home. He'd done his good deed and felt puffy-chested about it, too. Sang all the way home and got ready to warble with his mate, Netta. He carried on, "Tik, tik, tik," calling Netta. And he sang, "What-cheer, what-cheer!"

She heard him, too. Netta waited, but when she saw him, she didn't know who he was. For when Cardinal Red had left home before, he was gray-feathered everywhere on him. Her brownish-gray coat had matched him to a B.G., for brown and gray. Now, here he was back and awfully *red*!

"Get away, you scary thing!" Netta Gray hollered. She flew away, singing over her shoulder at him, "Cha-da—Cha-da-Cha! Away with you!"

Cardinal Red, he didn't know what to make of it. Hours went by, but he couldn't get Netta to sit still long enough to hear what he had to say for himself. She kept fluttering off.

She'd sing at him, "Cha-da—Cha-da-Cha!
Who are you? I don't know you. Go away, away!"

"Now, Netta, you know who I am," said poor Cardinal Red.
But she would flutter-fly, all upset, and singing:

"Oh, no, sir, you're much too red
on your wings, breast, and crest.
Oh, go away with you!"

To make matters worse, that swift runner and flyer, Plover Killdeer, came swooshing out of the woods just at sunset. She trilled and hollered at Cardinal Red, "Did you kill Bruh Deer? Did you, did you? Kill Deer? Kill Deer?"

"I haven't killed a thing!" said Cardinal Red. He kept trying to wipe off his blood-red feathers. But they were red, for true, and for good. "I helped Bruh Deer," said Cardinal Red. "And when I left him, he was alive, too." He chased off that nosey Plover Killdeer. And he hurried after Netta. He pestered her. He flashed his bright wings in front of her. He dashed at her. There was a race and chase through the woods with them.

He and Netta came out to the pond's edge. They were deep inside the dark pine trees now. And they stopped to breathe some air, they'd been pulling so hard. They looked into the pond. Cardinal had already touched her with his redness—feathers, wing, breast, and tail. And now, she looked just about as red as he. But not quite. No, there was some brownish left on her. But she could see she was enough like Cardinal Red to make up with him.

"Well, the wonder of it all," she said. "I am, like you, dear, some part *red*. I shall change my name. No more Netta Gray. From now on, I shall be known as Scarlet Red!" And so she was.

The two of them sat on a limb and sang together as pretty as they knew how. But still today, it makes Cardinal Red real upset when that noisy, nosey Plover Killdeer comes along out of the woods and swamp, yelling her head off, "Kill Deer! Kill Deer! You did, I know you did!"

Well, he sure didn't. Cardinal Red never hurt a soul.

And this advice I give to you, children, free of charge: *Don't change anything about you when you are far from home; that is, if you want a welcome when you get back!*

Little Brown Wren

Little Brown Wren lived in the corner where bushes grew together and the ends of fences met. She and her friend Winter Wren hopped around, deep in the brambles.

Brown Wren looked up; she could see the way-high sky up there. "Uh-huh, there it is," she told Winter Wren.

"There what is?" asked her friend.

"Up there, see? All the high-flyers are on the wing," Brown Wren told Winter Wren.

"Maybe so," said Winter Wren, "but I have to get to work." And off she went, flitting low from blackberry to dog rosebush, then scratching on the ground among the rocks.

Brown Wren was busy herself, seeing it all. Way up above was Bruh Eagle flying almost to the sun's eye. Bruh Buzzard was up there, too, so free-winging that he sailed himself among the clouds.

All of a sudden, Field Lark streaked up from the clover in the meadow. She twirled her wings so fast they looked like pin-wheels. Up and up to the sky Field Lark went, just as smooth as a duck on a pond.

Blue Jay and Bluebird, Mockingbird and Dove were watching the goings-on. Brown Wren spied them above her, perched in the apple tree. The big crowd of them gave her an idea. She'd make up a story, then boast about it. Brown Wren chattered loudly:

"Listen to me!
I see that we
can almost touch the sky.
Oh, my, yes! You and I!"

Now you know little Brown Wren and Winter Wren, too, never could fly any higher than a tall woman's shoulder. The birds in the apple tree were just shocked to hear her boast so.

Winter Wren fluttered over from the mulberry bush and said, "Now hush that noise, Brown Wren, before everybody laughs at you."

But little Brown Wren went right on, just as excited as she could be.

She said:

> *"Winter Wren,*
> *let's you and I*
> *just try to touch*
> *that great big sky!*
> *Let's show everybody!"*

All the other birds who were listening were screaming and whistling to one another about the little wren down there.

"She thinks she's equal to the size of Bruh Buzzard's wings! Big talk! B-i-i-i-g *talk*!" screeched Blue Jay.

Bird sounds rose on the air. Bruh Buzzard heard every word. He called down to the tree birds:

"Haw, haw,
   there's no law against tryin'
   this way-high-flyin'!"

And then Lark sang from the grass-tuft where she'd
dropped in a-dazement at Wren's boasting:

   "Pride will fill you full.
    Boasts will knock you over,
    but you can sure try to fly
    higher and higher."

Dove sat on a hawthorn bush and cooed
to Brown Wren:

   "Go on then!
    Show us what you can do.
    I'd try to fly it
    if I were you!"

The field sparrows who always fly low were upset over Brown
Wren's foolish words. Still, one of them called loudly, "Sis
Wren, you must be very brave then, to go high-flyin'. I say,
there's no harm in tryin'! Try it! Fly it!"

    Poor little Wren. Now she would have to try to fly high.
All the other birds clattered and cried, "Try! Fly! Go on,
up high!"

Brown Wren was only built for a hop, skip, and jump. Now she had to skip the hop and start as high as she could on the jump. She did it, too. Whoo-up she went.

And just as she did, there came a flash of fast wind. Oh, yes, it was! It slipped right under little Brown Wren. It lifted her right up over the top rail of the snake fence. It dashed her as high as the treetops. The wind carried on with Miss *Her*. Took her past Bruh Buzzard's range. It tossed her beyond Bruh Eagle's way. When Wren saw Bruh Eagle going by below her, she grew afraid for the very first time.

Just then, that wind that came from nowhere scooted out from under her. Brown Wren began to drop. Eagle gave her a soft slap with his wings to slow her down. She dropped to the buzzard's range, and he gave her a slappity-hold with *his* wing. When Wren kept coming down, Field Lark gave her a quick grab-flick as she fell by. When little Brown Wren reached the range of Jay, Redbird, and Pee-Wee, she was all ruffled and tussled from the slap-hold-flick. Poor thing scrambled back to her fence corner. Yes, she did too.

Redbird told her, "You've been sent back where you belong."

"You were born down there," said Blue Jay. "Get used to it."

Well, you know what they say. A streak of luck may lift up a self-praiser for a bit of time, but not for very long.

Children, I'll tell you true so you'll remember: *The braggart is much like a balloon full of air. One day soon, he's sure to burst!*

61

Afterword

Folktales are told over and over again, for years and years and even centuries. Sometimes the tales get so widely told that it is no longer possible to know who started them or where they came from. The stories in *When Birds Could Talk & Bats Could Sing* were first written down by Martha Young (1862–1941). Miss Young grew up on plantations where her father had kept slaves. She knew the black folk stories told by former slaves who, after the Civil War, were the paid house servants to her wealthy family.

Martha Young became Alabama's foremost folklorist, a collector of black folktales and songs and a writer of many such tales of her own in the African American tradition. She was known as an extraordinary "dialect interpreter." She became adept at the so-called black dialect of the Plantation Era. And like Joel Chandler Harris, writer of the *Uncle Remus* Brer Rabbit stories gathered from southern blacks, Miss Young also published her bird stories in local newspapers.

At this point in time, it is no longer possible to know which tales were of Martha Young's own creation and which were based on tales told by black tellers—first, those who were slaves when she was a little child, then, after Freedom, the household servants on the plantations owned by her father.

In any case, the bird and bat tales are uniquely imaginative. They are written in a prose style called *cante fable*, tales that include verse or song and end with a moral for children to live by.

The stories in *When Birds Could Talk & Bats Could Sing* were originally written in a heavy, tongue-twisting, so-called black dialect. I have recast and rewritten a choice few of them here in an easy-to-read colloquial speech. I have written them down especially for children, to make them smile. They are meant to be read aloud, too.

THE PAINTINGS FOR

WHEN BIRDS COULD TALK & BATS COULD SING

WERE EXECUTED IN TRANSPARENT WATERCOLOR

ON PAPER HANDMADE BY SIMON GREEN

AT THE BARCHAM GREEN PAPER MILLS

IN MAIDSTONE, KENT, GREAT BRITAIN, IN 1982

FOR THE ROYAL WATERCOLOUR SOCIETY.

•

THE TEXT TYPE IS STONE SERIF MEDIUM

DESIGNED BY SUMNER STONE IN 1987

FOR ADOBE SYSTEMS, MOUNTAIN VIEW, CALIFORNIA.

THE DISPLAY TYPE IS DIOTIMA ITALIC

DESIGNED BY GUDRUN ZAPF VON HESSE IN 1953

FOR THE STEMPEL FOUNDRY, FRANKFURT, GERMANY.

THE TYPE WAS SET BY WLCR NEW YORK, INC.

THE TITLE WAS HANDLETTERED BY REASSURANCE WUNDER,

BASED ON DIOTIMA ITALIC.

MR. WUNDER'S CURRENT DOMICILE IS UNKNOWN.

HE WAS LAST SEEN IN MAYFIELD, KENTUCKY.

•

COLOR SEPARATIONS WERE MADE

BY BRIGHT LIGHTS, LTD., SINGAPORE.

PRINTED AND BOUND BY TIEN WAH PRESS, SINGAPORE

PRODUCTION SUPERVISION BY ANGELA BIOLA

DESIGNED BY BARRY MOSER AND KATHLEEN WESTRAY